The Snowman

Cynthia Rider • Alex Brychta

OXFORD

UNIVERSITY PRESS

Biff   Chip   Wilma

Wilf   Kipper   Floppy

Wilma made a snowman.

It had a red nose.

It had a blue scarf.

It had green gloves.

It had a black hat.

The hat fell on Floppy.

Floppy ran.

Oh no!

No snowman!

Think about the story

What are the colours the snowman is wearing?

Why did Floppy run off?

What else could you put on the snowman?

What would you like to make with snow or sand?

Fun activity

Find the twin snowmen.

Useful common words repeated in this story and other books at Level 1.

a   had   it   no

Names in this story: Biff   Chip   Kipper   Wilf   Wilma   Floppy